ABOUT THE BANK STREET READY-TO-READ SERIES

Seventy years of educational research and innovative teaching have given the Bank Street College of Education the reputation as America's most trusted name in early childhood education.

Because no two children are exactly alike in their development, we have designed the *Bank Street Ready-to-Read* series in three levels to accommodate the individual stages of reading readiness of children ages four through eight.

- ○ *Level 1:* GETTING READY TO READ—read-alouds for children who are taking their first steps toward reading.
- ● *Level 2:* READING TOGETHER—for children who are just beginning to read by themselves but may need a little help.
- ○ *Level 3:* I CAN READ IT MYSELF—for children who can read independently.

Our three levels make it easy to select the books most appropriate for a child's development and enable him or her to grow with the series step by step. The *Bank Street Ready-to-Read* books also overlap and reinforce each other, further encouraging the reading process.

We feel that making reading fun and enjoyable is the single most important thing that you can do to help children become good readers. And we hope you'll be a part of Bank Street's long tradition of learning through sharing.

The Bank Street College of Education

For J.R.
— W.H.H.

For Cassandra
— R.W.A.

WHERE'S LULU?
A Bantam Little Rooster Book
Simultaneous paper-over-board and trade paper editions / June 1991

Little Rooster is a trademark of Bantam Books,
a division of Bantam Doubleday Dell Publishing Group, Inc.

Series graphic design by Alex Jay/Studio J
Associate Editor: Gillian Bucky

Special thanks to James A. Levine, Betsy Gould,
Erin B. Gathrid, and Cheryl Dixon.

Library of Congress Cataloging-in-Publication Data
Hooks, William H.
Where's Lulu? / by William H. Hooks;
illustrated by R. W. Alley.
p.   cm.—(Bank Street ready-to-read)
"A Byron Preiss book."
"A Bantam little rooster book."
Summary: Just when Lulu the dog is needed
to help play catch with the new ball
from Dad, she cannot be found.
ISBN 0-553-07093-2.—ISBN 0-553-35211-3 (pbk.)
[1. Dogs—Fiction.] I. Alley, R. W. (Robert W.), ill.
II. Title. III. Series.
PZ7.H7664Wh 1991
[E]—dc20
90-31815 CIP AC

Published simultaneously in the United States and Canada

Bantam Books are published by Bantam Books, a division of Bantam Doubleday
Dell Publishing Group, Inc. Its trademark, consisting of the words "Bantam Books"
and the portrayal of a rooster, is Registered in U.S. Patent and Trademark Office
and in other countries. Marca Registrada. Bantam Books, 666 Fifth Avenue, New
York, New York 10103.

PRINTED IN THE UNITED STATES OF AMERICA

0 9 8 7 6 5 4 3 2 1

Where's Lulu?

by William H. Hooks
Illustrated by R. W. Alley

A Byron Preiss Book

A BANTAM LITTLE ROOSTER BOOK

NEW YORK · TORONTO · LONDON · SYDNEY · AUCKLAND

I found the ball
when I woke up.
It was on the table by my bed.
There was a note on it.
It read:
      For my best pal.
        Love,
        Dad

"Hey, Dad is home," I yelled.
I picked up the ball
and ran down the hall.
"Hey, Dad, this is great!"
I called.
"Can we play catch?"

Mom met me in the hall.
"Shhh," she said.
"Dad is still asleep.
His plane was late."
"Okay," I said.
"Then I'll play with Lulu."

I got dressed
and went downstairs.
"Where's Lulu?" I asked Mom.
"In the kitchen," she said.

I went to the kitchen.
No Lulu.
Only Sam was there,
stuffing his face.
Sam is no fun.
He never wants to play
with me.
"Where's Lulu?" I asked.
"Watching TV," said Sam.

I went into the den.
No Lulu.
Only Sara was there,
watching *Mr. Rogers.*
Sara is too little to play catch.
"Where's Lulu?" I asked.
"She hates *Mr. Rogers*,"
said Sara.
"She went to Bebo's room."

I went to Bebo's room.
No Lulu.
Only Bebo was there,
crunching crackers
all over the floor.
"Where's Lulu?" I asked.
"Da-da-da," said Bebo,
pointing toward the window.
"She went outside?" I asked.
Bebo said, "Da-da-da!"

I went outside and called,
"Lulu, where are you?"
No answer.
"Hey, Lulu," I shouted.
"Dad gave me a new ball.
Let's play catch!"
Still no answer from Lulu.

Mrs. Long called to me,
"You shouldn't play
with matches."
She doesn't hear too well.
"No, Mrs. Long," I said.
"I was looking for Lulu
to play *catch*."
"Oh, Lulu," said Mrs. Long.
"I saw her go down
to the cellar."

I went down to the cellar.
No Lulu.
Only Grandpa was there,
sawing a board.
"Where's Lulu?" I asked.
"She hates the sound
the saw makes," said Grandpa.
"She left just a minute ago."

I went outside again.
I stood in the yard and yelled,
"Lulu, where are you?"
Still no Lulu.

So I started bouncing the ball
against the fence.
Thump! Catch!—
Thump! Catch!—

Suddenly, I heard running.
I kept on throwing my ball.
Thump! Catch!
Thump . . .
Catch!

Lulu caught the ball!
Lulu ran around and around
with the ball in her mouth.

I ran after her.
We both got dizzy
and fell on the grass.

Dad came out.
"Can I join you?"
he asked.

So we played three-way catch
all morning.
Can you guess who
never missed a ball?
Lulu!

William H. Hooks is the author of many books for children, including the highly acclaimed *Moss Gown* and, most recently, *The Three Little Pigs and the Fox*. He is also the Director of Publications at Bank Street College. As part of Bank Street's Media Group, he has been closely involved with such projects as the well-known Bank Street Readers and Discoveries: An Individualized Reading Program. Mr. Hooks lives with three cats in a Greenwich Village brownstone in New York City.

R. W. Alley studied at Haverford College and has been illustrating children's books since 1981. He is the author-illustrator of *The Clever Carpenter* and *Watch Out, Cyrus!*, as well as the illustrator of many other children's books including *The Legend of Sleepy Hollow* and *Mrs. Toggle's Zipper*. Mr. Alley lives with his wife and baby daughter in Rhode Island.